P9-BJB-507

Love You,
Keillor ❤
♥ BUNNY ♥

GUESS
HOW MUCH
I LOVE YOU

To Liz with love,
A. J.

Text copyright © 1994 by Sam McBratney
Illustrations copyright © 1994 by Anita Jeram

Guess How Much I Love You™ is a registered
trademark of Walker Books Ltd., London

All rights reserved. No part of this book may be reproduced, transmitted,
or stored in an information retrieval system in any form or by any means,
graphic, electronic, or mechanical, including photocopying, taping, and
recording, without prior written permission from the publisher.

First U.S. edition in this format 2009

Library of Congress Cataloging-in-Publication Data
McBratney, Sam.
Guess how much I love you / by Sam McBratney ;
illustrated by Anita Jeram. — 1st U.S. ed.
Summary: During a bedtime game, every time Little Nutbrown Hare
demonstrates how much he loves his father, Big Nutbrown Hare
gently shows him that the love is returned even more.
ISBN 978-1-56402-473-2 (reinforced trade ed.)
[1. Hares—Fiction. 2. Fathers and sons—Fiction. 3. Bedtime—Fiction.
4. Love—Fiction.] I. Jeram, Anita, ill. II. Title.
PZ7.M47826Gu 1995
[E]—dc20 94-001599
ISBN 978-0-7636-4913-5 (gift edition)

14 15 12 11 10 09
LGO 10 9 8 7 6 5 4 3 2 1

Printed in Venice, Italy

This book was typeset in Cochin.
The illustrations in this book were done in watercolor and ink.

Candlewick Press
99 Dover Street
Somerville, Massachusetts 02144

visit us at www.candlewick.com

GUESS HOW MUCH I LOVE YOU

by
Sam McBratney

illustrated by
Anita Jeram

CANDLEWICK PRESS

Little Nutbrown Hare, who was going to bed, held on tight to Big Nutbrown Hare's very long ears.

bunny ← *When I read I'll say your favorite "bunny*

He wanted to be sure that Big
Nutbrown Bunny ~~Hare~~ was listening.
"Guess how much
I love you," he said.

"Oh, I don't think I could guess that,"
said Big Nutbrown Hare.

"This much," said Little
 Nutbrown Hare, stretching out
 his arms as wide as they could go.

Big Nutbrown Hare had even
longer arms. "But I love *you*
this much," he said.

Hmm, that is a lot, thought
Little Nutbrown Hare.

"I love you
as high as
I can reach,"
said Little
Nutbrown
Hare.

"I love you
as high as
I can reach,"
said Big
Nutbrown
Hare.

That is very
high, thought
Little Nutbrown
Hare. I wish
I had arms
like that.

Then Little
Nutbrown Hare
had a good idea.
He tumbled
upside down
and reached
up the tree
trunk with
his feet.

"I love you
all the way up
to my toes!"
he said.

"And *I* love you
all the way up
to your toes," said
Big Nutbrown Hare,
swinging him up
over his head.

"I love you
  as high as
I can hop!"
  laughed Little
    Nutbrown Hare,

bouncing up
    and down.

"But I love you as high as
I can hop," smiled Big
Nutbrown Hare—and he
hopped so high that his ears
touched the branches above.

That's good
hopping,
thought
Little
Nutbrown
Hare.
I wish I
could hop
like that.

"I love you all the way down the
lane as far as the river," cried
Little Nutbrown Hare.

"I love you across the river
and over the hills," said
Big Nutbrown Hare.

That's very far, thought
Little Nutbrown Hare.
He was almost too sleepy
to think anymore.

Then he looked beyond the
thornbushes, out into the big
dark night. Nothing could
be farther than the sky.

"I love you right up to
the moon," he said,
and closed his eyes.

"Oh, that's far," said
Big Nutbrown Hare.
"That is very,
very far."

Big Nutbrown Hare settled
Little Nutbrown Hare
into his bed of leaves.

He leaned over
and kissed him
good night.

Then he lay down close by
and whispered with a smile,
"I love you right up to the moon—

and back."

I Love You
Keillor
<....This much ~...>
Mimi
2011